TIGGER
AND FRIENDS

by DENNIS HAMLEY

Illustrations by
Meg Rutherford

LOTHROP, LEE & SHEPARD BOOKS
NEW YORK

For the cats themselves

Text copyright © 1988 by Dennis Hamley
Illustrations copyright © 1988 by Meg Rutherford
First published in 1988 by André Deutsch Limited
All rights reserved. No part of this book may be reproduced or utilized in any
form or by any means, electronic or mechanical, including photocopying,
recording or by any information storage and retrieval system, without permission
in writing from the Publisher. Inquiries should be addressed to Lothrop, Lee &
Shepard Books, a division of William Morrow & Company, Inc., 105 Madison
Avenue, New York, New York 10016.
First U.S. Edition   1989   1 2 3 4 5 6 7 8 9 10

Library of Congress Cataloging-in-Publication Data
Hamley, Dennis.   Tigger and friends.
Summary: A pugnacious cat named Tigger learns to share his house with another
cat, who is gentle and friendly, and this spirit of cooperativeness becomes useful
to Tigger later in his life.   [1. Cats—Fiction]   I. Rutherford, Meg, ill.
II. Title.   PZ7.H18294Ti   1989   [E]   88-8385
ISBN 0-688-08606-3   ISBN 0-688-08605-5 (lib. bdg.)
Printed in Belgium by Proost International Book Production

Tigger was a brown Burmese cat. For twelve weeks after he was born, Tigger had to fight his brothers and sisters for what he got. Then one day some people came with a wicker cat basket and took Tigger away with them. They took him to a house where he was the only cat. Tigger was very happy.

Three months later, Tigger had a nasty surprise. His people brought the cat basket into the room, and a kitten crept out. Tigger was furious. He hissed and growled and scratched and bit. The new kitten mewed and hid under the sofa. Tigger felt good. He was boss.

The new kitten's name was Thomas. He was tiny and round, with gray eyes that matched his gray fur. Tigger was sure he could get rid of him any time he liked, but Thomas kept coming back for more. After a week, Tigger had a terrible thought. *Thomas wasn't going to go away.*

Even worse, Tigger's people seemed to like Thomas. How could this be? His people weren't supposed to like anyone except him. Tigger curled up in the closet to think things over. What was the point of scaring the life out of Thomas if his people liked him?

Next morning, Tigger was eating his breakfast. He was enjoying it. Then suddenly a small gray head pushed under his chin. Thomas was stealing his food. Tigger got ready to be angry, but he wasn't angry. Tigger didn't mind sharing his food with Thomas.

Days, weeks, and months went by. Tigger enjoyed being friends with Thomas. Thomas never tried to be boss. When they had a fight, Tigger won. If Tigger climbed a tree, Thomas sat below and watched. If Tigger wanted the best chair or nearest lap, Thomas sat somewhere else.

Thomas grew big and fat. His eyes turned green. Tigger stayed small and lean.

Tigger and Thomas made a good pair.

A dreadful day came. Tigger went out onto the main road and got too close to a car. The vet had to take off his left front leg. Tigger had to learn to walk on just three legs. Thomas helped. He washed Tigger's face where the one paw wouldn't reach. He let Tigger fight him so his one front paw would become strong.

The vet said Tigger's front leg would become strong enough to knock out other cats with one blow. The vet was right. Tigger went on fighting, and Thomas went on watching. Tigger was happy because he was still boss. Thomas was happy because he wasn't. Thomas knew his place – in the warm with his tummy full.

Years went by. Then one morning Tigger lay in a sunny patch on the carpet. He yawned and listened to the voices of his people outside. They were calling Thomas. Tigger went to sleep. Far away, he could hear the voices of his people. Calling, calling. Calling Thomas.

Tigger dreamed that he was out in the garden. His people were standing in a circle. They were looking at a patch of ground that had just been dug. Thomas was not there.

In his dream, Tigger was frightened. He woke up. The sun had gone behind a cloud. He listened. He could hear his people. Not calling, but crying.

Tigger ran outside, into the garden. In the corner, where his people had been in his dream, the earth was newly dug. Why was that wooden cross there? Where was Thomas?

He went back into the house. His people picked him up and made a fuss over him. Tigger struggled to be free. There was a smell on their hands that he did not know. It frightened him.

Tigger walked around the house and around the garden, calling for Thomas. But Thomas never came.

The days went by. Tigger had to curl up in the closet by himself. There was no one to steal his food and no one to fight with. Some people say that cats don't get lonely. But Tigger was.

Slowly the memory of his big fat friend grew dim. Tigger still called, the way he used to call Thomas for a fight, but he had forgotten who was supposed to come. He curled up in the closet to think about it. Tigger was very sad, but he was only a cat and didn't know why.

One afternoon Tigger's people brought in the wicker cat basket and put it on the carpet. One of his people came over and stroked him. The other opened the basket. Tigger could not believe his eyes at what came out.

It was a very tiny creature. It had a sharp brown face, big brown ears, a long brown tail, and brown feet. All the rest of it was cream color. Its eyes were big, deep, and blue.

The creature opened its mouth. What a screech! Tigger's back fur stood up, and his tail fluffed out. He let out a furious hiss. The strong hands holding him stopped stroking and held him back. Tigger wanted to go after the intruder at once.

Tigger stalked out of the house. He had to get away. He curled
up in the garden shed next door to think about it. He did not come
home again until it was dark. A memory stirred. Yes, this was just
as it had been once before – *his people seemed to like the little creature.*

Now Tigger could remember Thomas, and this creature was not the least bit like him. She didn't seem to know who was boss. She ran rings around him and made him giddy. When he waved his tail, she jumped on it. If he took his eyes off her for a second, she stole all the food from his plate. No, she wasn't like Thomas at all.

Tigger curled up in the closet to think about it. His people had named her Claudia. What sort of name for a cat was Claudia?

Tigger decided that Claudia would have to go, but how? He looked down at the trusty right paw that Thomas had helped to make strong. *All right, Miss Claudia*, he thought. *You're going to get yours*. Then Tigger curled his paw over his face and went happily to sleep.

Next morning, Claudia ate half his breakfast. Tigger had to have another bowl in the next room. Then he sat on the sunny patch on the carpet to wash himself. Claudia jumped on his tail. Tigger tried to walk with dignity through the open back door. Claudia pushed past him.

That did it. Tigger hissed. He snarled. His tail fluffed out. He rocked back on his kangaroo hind legs and lifted his paw. With claws out, he let go a lightning right hook to the head. He caught Claudia on the ear. She cried and ran away.

Tigger walked on. He was pleased with himself. He was boss again. That's what Claudia could expect all the time now.

Tigger found her hiding under a bush. Her left ear was flat on her head. Yes, he had hurt her all right. Good.

Then Tigger remembered the day he had returned home with just three legs. What had gentle Thomas done that day? Tigger leaned forward and licked Claudia's ear where it was hurt. Claudia purred. Tigger thought, *I can't stand her, but she seems to like me.*

And she did. Wherever Tigger went, Claudia followed. She tried to take over all his favorite places. Some Tigger didn't mind about. Others he never went near again.

Tigger wasn't lonely anymore, but he wasn't happy either. One day, he curled up in the closet to think about it.

And this is what he thought:
What am I going to do about her?
She never stops running and jumping.
She gets in my way all the time.
She won't leave me alone.
I'm too old for this.
He sighed, then closed his eyes and slept.

He woke and opened one eye. A gray shadow lay beside him. A rough tongue licked his head. Tigger purred. His old companion had returned – just for one second. But in that second Tigger heard Thomas say, *Be nice to her, old friend. She's just like we were once.* And then Tigger was alone again in the closet.

When Tigger came back out into the room, Claudia bounded up to him. He lifted his paw, ready to hit. Then he stopped. *All right, Thomas*, he thought, and licked Claudia's face. Claudia purred. To his surprise, so did Tigger. He lay down to consider this new feeling.

Things won't ever be as they were before, he thought. *But they needn't be too bad. I can try to like her.* And try he did, for all the contented years he had left. Perhaps, though – just once or twice – Thomas had to come back for a second or two, to keep Tigger up to it.